Mel Bay Presents

The Hammered Dulcimer Treasury of Tunes

Arrangements by
Sally Hawley

Cover photo by John Baldwin (www.fpstudio.com)
Music typesetting by Sally Hawley.

2 3 4 5 6 7 8 9 0

Visit us on the Web at www.melbay.com — E-mail us at email@melbay.com

Sally Hawley

Photography: George Hawley, Tom Conley
Hammered Dulcimer on cover built by Ray Epler.

This book is dedicated
to the memory of my
beloved husband,

George P. Hawley

Table of Contents

Section 1
Oldtime Traditional Tunes

Section 2
Celtic Traditional Tunes

Traditional Music

The term "Traditional Music" can mean many things to many people. However, the true definition of "tradition" is the handing down of customs, beliefs, etc. from generation to generation, or refers to a long established custom that has the effect of an unwritten law. The term "Folk Music" can be interpreted to mean traditional music, or later music performed in the traditional style. Music of the 1960s is now considered by many as folk music.

Actual traditional music was passed down vocally, or learned by ear instrumentally, and derived from countries where our ancestors originated. In the heartland of the United States, British Isles traditional music is much appreciated, as many of our ancestors came from England, Ireland, Scotland, Wales and Briton. Trying to separate American and Celtic traditional music is an impossible task, as so many of the tunes we consider our own, are adapted versions of tunes passed on to us from other countries and would fit into either category. For my old-time book, I have selected tunes which are commonly heard at gatherings of old-time musicians.

Many traditional tunes were composed not for financial gain, but for amusement and dancing. Often they were written by well established and famous composers at a time when the distinction between popular and classic music was nonexistent. Even the great Handel wrote tunes performed in both homes and taverns. Therefore, many tunes in the public domain may well have been the products of composers noted in their day. Also, traditional music is living proof that music does not have to be complicated or difficult to play for true entertainment.

Many royal family members were musicians and collectors of traditional music, such as King Henry VIII, Elizabeth I, and Lady Jane. Samuel Pepys mentions many traditional tunes in his famous diary, and Thomas Jefferson enjoyed traditional music. We are grateful to Francis O'Neill of West Cork, Ireland who immigrated to Chicago at age 16, and in the early 1900s compiled and documented in standard notation one of the largest collections of Irish traditional tunes.

The Hammered Dulcimer

The hammered dulcimer is a member of the zither family in which sound is produced by the vibration of strings stretched across a wooden soundboard. This forerunner of the harpsichord and piano is a trapezoid shaped instrument with 46 - 78 or more sets of strings which are struck with mallets. It is also a first cousin to the psaltery of the same shape on which the strings are plucked.

Originating in the middle eastern countries, it traveled into Europe during the time of the crusades, and was widely accepted during the Medieval and Renaissance periods. Today the instrument still exists in all parts of the world, as the Greek santouri, Swiss hackbrett, Hungarian cymbalom, Chinese yangchen, Italian dolcemia, Indian and Persian santuri, and English and American hammered dulcimer.

Brought to the colonies by immigrants from the British Isles and Europe, it was very popular on the frontier due to its portability and adaptability for traditional music. During the 19th Century its use declined. However, today the hammered dulcimer is being produced and enjoyed by a heritage conscious generation that has rediscovered its enchanting sound.

Sally (Hunter) Hawley, a multi-talented musician and artist, has been involved in music for a lifetime. Growing up during the depression years in a small town in southern Indiana, the daughter of a music teacher and barbershop quartet singer, music was an integral part of home entertainment.

During the 1960s, after transferring with her husband and family to West Virginia, she first heard the enchanting sounds of the mountain and hammered dulcimers, and learned to play from area oldtime musicians. She has become an accomplished player with a wide repertoire, and has traveled across the country performing at fairs and special events, and studying as well as teaching at dulcimer festivals. Through the years, Sally has collected hundreds of traditional tunes, and began documenting her arrangements in standard notation for her students, hoping to help preserve this legacy of music for the enjoyment of future generations.

Four recordings of her traditional music are available: "*Heirlooms & Keepsakes*", "*Something Old and Something New*", "*Timeless Treasures*", and "*Perennial Pleasures*". In addition, there is a CD with the "Presby Pickers", a band she performs with, titled "*The Spirit Of The Mountains*". Contact Hawley Studios at dulcisally2@aol.com.

Playing The Symbols and Ornamentation

The hammered dulcimer adapts itself well to playing traditional music, much of which is based on a diatonic scale (do re me fa sol la ti do).

There are many styles and types of hammers made and preferred by various players. I have tried many of these, and recommend each player to experiment with many before deciding on anything. Try flexible, firm, wrapped, bowed, curled, padded, etc., until you find the hammers that feel most comfortable to you, and with which you are able to express your music and style. I have settled on the firm, shaped wood hammers with cupped end, with and without leather padding, depending on the sound I want to put forth.

The following music symbols are commonly used in folk and traditional music. You will find them in my arrangements. I use them in the following manner, and they are accomplished by the hammered dulcimist as below:

2 SLASHES:
Written as: Play as:

One quarter note sounded as two eighth notes.

Holding the hammers firmly between thumb and forefinger, with wrists flexible, strike the note allowing it to bounce twice with equal timing. Stop further bouncing by compressing the second finger resting beneath the hammer handle. I usually try to do this with the right hand.

MORDENT:

Written as: Play as:

One quarter note played as multiples.

Holding hammer loosely, strike strings with a strong stroke allowing the hammer to bounce 3-4 times, according to the timing allotment.

GRACE NOTE:

Written as: Play as noted.

A quick, softer, higher note played before the actual note, used often in Scottish and Irish music.

Use either right or left hammer for light tap on higher note, then with alternate hammer, strike the actual note.

FLAM:

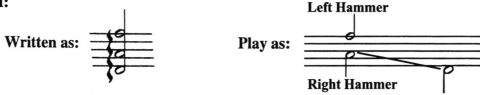

Written as: **Play as:**

Look carefully at the strings on your dulcimer, and make a mental note of the spot where the strings on the treble bridge form a "V" with the strings on the bass bridge. Simultaneously, use left hammer to strike the highest of the notes on the left side of the treble bridge, and the right hammer to strike the middle note on the right side of the treble bridge. Then with a continuous movement and quick twist of your right wrist to the right and down slightly, allow the hammer to bounce to that spot, just past the right side of that "V" to the lowest of the notes on the bass bridge. With a little practice, this will become easy to accomplish, and it adds so much to your performance.

TURN or 5 Note Roll:

Written as: **Play as:**

This is an ornamentation used often in Irish music, giving it that very distinctive sound and rhythm. The symbol is easy to write, but a little more difficult to play. Position both hands close together and with the left hammer strike the note firmly, then with the right hammer, immediately strike the note above with sufficient force to bounce/drag the hammer down to the note itself, then the note below. Finish the turn, or roll, by again striking the note itself with the left hammer. You have now played a five note roll. Beginning with a left, a right drag down three notes, then another left.

MORDENT/SLASH:

Written as: **Play as:**

Using both left and right hammers, alternate playing the two notes in tremolo fashion for the timing length of the note.

ARPEGGIO:

Written as: **Play as:**

Alternating left and right hammers, starting with the lowest note, strike with enough force to allow each note to sustain as the following notes are sounded. Hammered dulcimers are very harmonic with this application. Reverse arpeggios are played the same, beginning with the highest to the lowest note.

TRIPLET:

Written as: **Play as noted.**

Three notes played in the timing of one note. Strike the highest of the notes with either right or left hammer with enough power to continue dragging the hammer down to the following two notes.

SOFT SUSTAIN:

ss

Written as: **Play as:**

This is not an actual music symbol, but one I have come up with to indicate sustained notes for my hammered dulcimer arrangements. I find many times while playing, the tone is not sustained long enough with one strike to complete the music notation, and needs a little soft nudge with the hammer to keep it going. Therefore, I have invented the symbol "ss". It is included in a few of my arrangements.

Section 1
Oldtime Traditional Tunes

ALLEMANDE SWISS

Arr. by S. J. Hawley

English Country Dance

ANGELINA BAKER

Arr. by S. J. Hawley

Oldtime Traditional

ANGLEWORM WIGGLE

Arr. by S. J. Hawley
Learned at Evart, Michigan Festival

Oldtime Traditional

ARKANSAS TRAVELER

Arr. by S. J. Hawley

Oldtime Reel

THE BELLES OF LEXINGTON

Arr. by S. J. Hawley
Learned from Melvin Wine

Oldtime Traditional

BILL CHEATHAM

Arr. by S. J. Hawley
Learned from Worley Gardner

Traditional Oldtime

BILLY IN THE LOWGROUND

Arr. by S.J.Hawley

Traditional Oldtime

BIRDIE

Arr. by S. J. Hawley

American Oldtime Traditional

BLACKBERRY BLOSSOM

Arr. by S. J. Hawley

Oldtime Traditional

BLACK VELVET WALTZ

Arr. by S. J. Hawley
Learned from Al Leitz in Michigan

Traditional

BONAPARTE CROSSING THE RHINE

Arr. by S. J. Hawley

Oldtime Traditional

BONAPARTE'S RETREAT

Arr. by S. J. Hawley

Oldtime Traditional

BREAKING UP CHRISTMAS

Learned from Dick Knowles

Oldtime Traditional

BROWN BUTTON SHOES

Arr. by S. J. Hawley
Learned from Dave Bing

Oldtime Traditional

BULL PUP

Arr. by S.J.Hawley
As learned from Worley Gardner

Oldtime Traditional

BUNKER HILL

Arr. by S. J. Hawley
Learned from Jim Ruziska

Oldtime Traditional

Embellished Version:

CEDAR LAKES SHUFFLE

S. J. Hawley   **Oldtime Traditional Style**

Mountain State Arts & Craft Fair, Cedar Lakes Convention Center, Ripley, West Virginia.

THE CHEROKEE SHUFFLE

Arr. by S. J. Hawley
Learned from Lefty Shafer

Oldtime Traditional

THE CHEROKEE SHUFFLE

Arr. by S. J. Hawley
Try it in the Key of D

Oldtime Traditional

CHICKEN REEL

Arr. by S. J. Hawley

American Traditional

CHINESE BREAKDOWN

Arr. by S. J. Hawley

Oldtime Traditional

CINDY

Arr. by S. J. Hawley

Oldtime Traditional

Oh I wish I was an ap - ple, a hang-in' in the tree, And

ev - ery time my sweet-heart passed, she'd take a bite of me, She

told me that she loved me, she called me sug - ar plum, She

threw her arms a - round me, I - tho't my time had come.

Get a-long home, Cin - dy, Cin - dy, Get a-long home, Cin - dy, Cin - dy,

Get a - long home Cin - dy, Cin - dy, I'll mar - ry you some day.

COLD FROSTY MORNING

Arr. by S. J. Hawley

Oldtime Traditional

Alternate Version:

COME DANCE AND SING

Arr. by S. J. Hawley

New England Traditional

Cabin Creek Quilts, Malden, West Virginia.

COTTON EYED JOE

Arr. by S. J. Hawley

Oldtime Traditional

CRIPPLE CREEK

Arr. by S. J. Hawley

Traditional Oldtime

Go - in down to Crip - ple Creek, Go - in' on the run,

Go - in' down to Crip - ple Creek to have a lit - tle fun. Oh fun, oh

Go - in' down to Crip - ple go - in' bout a mile,

Go - in' down to Crip - ple Creek to see my lit - tle

VARIATION:

CUCKOO'S NEST

Arr. by S. J. Hawley
Learned from Sam Rizzetta

Arr. by S. J. Hawley
Learned from Sam Rizzetta

Oldtime Traditional

Dupont High School Campus, Belle, West Virginia.

THE CUMBERLAND GAP

Arr. by S. J. Hawley

Oldtime Traditional

CURTSY TO YOUR PARTNER

Arr. for Hammered Dulcimer

S. J. Hawley
Oldtime Traditional Style

THE DEVIL AMONG THE YEARLINGS

Arr. by S. J. Hawley
Learned from Bobby Taylor

Oldtime Traditional Reel

DEVIL'S DREAM

Arr. by S. J. Hawley

Oldtime Traditional Reel

New Fort Salem Dulcimer Festival, Salem, West Virginia.

DEVIL'S TEA TABLE

Arr. for Hammered Dulcimer
Rock formation near Worthington, Indiana

S. J. Hawley
Oldtime Style

DOWN BY THE GARDEN GATE

Arr. by S. J. Hawley
Learned from Melvin Wine

Oldtime Traditional Waltz

EBENEZER

Arr. by S. J. Hawley
Learned at Vandalia Gathering

Oldtime Traditional Reel
Also called "West Virginia Highway"

THE EIGHTH OF JANUARY

Arr. by S. J. Hawley

Oldtime Reel

New Fort Salem Dulcimer Festival, Salem, West Virginia.

ELZIC'S FAREWELL

Arr. by S. J. Hawley
Learned from David Gladkosky

Oldtime Traditional

FISHER'S HORNPIPE

Arr. by S. J. Hawley

Irish and Oldtime Traditional

FLOP EARED MULE

Arr. by S. J. Hawley

Oldtime Traditional

Alternate Part B:

FLY AROUND MY PRETTY LITTLE MISS

Arr. by S. J. Hawley

Oldtime Traditional Reel

Vandalia Gathering, WV State Cultural Center, Charleston, West Virginia.

FLYING CLOUD COTILLION

Arr. by S. J. Hawley

New England Traditional Reel

FOGGY RIVER

Arr. for Hammered Dulcimer

S. J. Hawley
Oldtime Style

The Presby Pickers at Highlawn Presbyterian Church, St. Albans, West Virginia.

FOLDING DOWN THE SHEETS

Arr. by S. J. Hawley

Oldtime Traditional

FORKED DEER

Arr. by S. J. Hawley

Oldtime Traditional

GARY OWEN

Arr. by S. J. Hawley

Irish and Oldtime Traditional
Played for the charge at Custer's Last Stand

GEORGE'S JIG

S. J. Hawley

Irish Traditional Style

Stonewall Jackson's Mill Jubilee, Weston, West Virginia.

GLORY IN THE MEETING HOUSE

Learned from Richard Knowles
Augusta Repertoire Class

Oldtime Traditional

GOLDEN SLIPPERS

Arr. by S. J. Hawley

Oldtime Traditional

The Presby Pickers, Highlawn Presbyterian Church, St. Albans, West Virginia.

GOODBYE LIZA JANE

Arr. by S. J. Hawley
Learned from Glen Smith

Oldtime Traditional Reel

63

GRANNY WILL YOUR DOG BITE

Arr. by S. J. Hawley

Oldtime Traditional

GREEN WILLIS

Arr. by S. J. Hawley
Learned from Ron and Nancy Utt at Prickett's Fort

Oldtime Traditional

HARVEST HOME

Arr. by S. J. Hawley

Irish and Oldtime Traditional

Begin with Left hammer, then alternate with right across treble bridge

Jam at the Conrad, WV State Folk Festival, Glenville, West Virginia.

HOME SWEET HOME

Arr. by S. J. Hawley

American Oldtime Traditional
H. Bishop

INDIANA HOE DOWN

Arr. by S. J. Hawley

Oldtime Traditional

I WONDER AS I WANDER

Arr. by S. J. Hawley

Part of the "Presby Pickers" historical program.

Ancient Traditional Tune

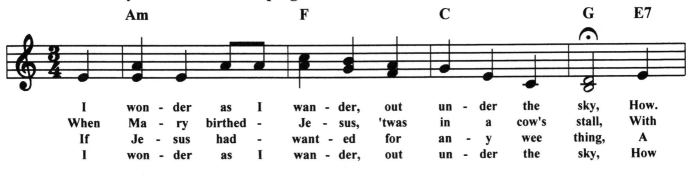

I won - der as I wan - der, out un - der the sky, How.
When Ma - ry birthed - Je - sus, 'twas in a cow's stall, With
If Je - sus had - want - ed for an - y wee thing, A
I won - der as I wan - der, out un - der the sky, How

Je - sus the Sav - iour did come for to die, For
wise men and farm - ers and shep - herds and all, But
star in the sky, or a bird on the wing, Or
Je - sus the Sav - iour did come for to die, For

poor, orn - ery peo - ple like you and like I, I
high from God's hea - ven a star's light did fall, and.the
all of God's ang - els in hea - ven to sing, He
poor orn - ery peo - ple like you and like I; I

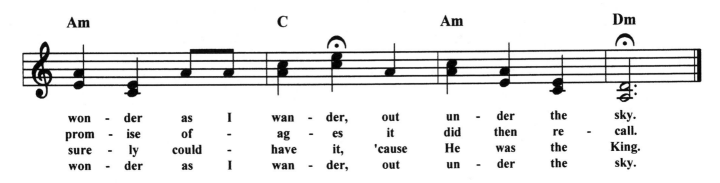

won - der as I wan - der, out un - der the sky.
prom - ise of - ag - es it did then re - call.
sure - ly could - have it, 'cause He was the King.
won - der as I wan - der, out un - der the sky.

JAYBIRD

Arr. by S. J. Hawley
Simple Version

Traditional Oldtime Reel

JAYBIRD

Arr. by S. J. Hawley
Variation and Embellishments

Traditional Oldtime Reel

JENNY LIND POLKA

Arr. by S. J. Hawley
Learned from Worley Gardner

Arr. by S. J. Hawley
Learned from Worley Gardner

American Oldtime Traditional

Stonewall Jackson's Mill Jubilee, Weston, West Virginia.

JOE PYE WEED

E Minor Reel

S. J. Hawley
Oldtime Style

JOYS OF QUEBEC

Arr. by S. J. Hawley

Canadian Traditional

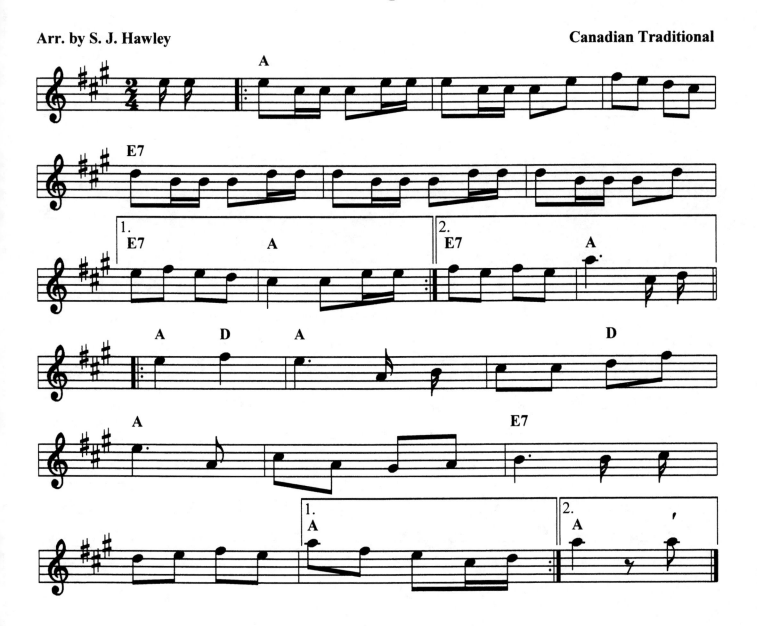

KEEP THE OLD ARK A'MOVERIN'

Arr. by S. J. Hawley

Traditional

As interpreted from Melvin Wine

LA BELLE CATHERINE

Arr. by S.J.Hawley
Learned from Worley Gardner

Oldtime Traditional

LEATHER BRITCHES

Arr. by S. J. Hawley
Learned at the Vandalia Gathering

Oldtime Traditional Reel

LIBERTY

Arr. by S.J.Hawley
The bare essentials.

Traditional Oldtime

LIBERTY

Arr. by S. J. Hawley
With embellishments

Oldtime Traditional

LI'L LIZA JANE

Arr. by S. J. Hawley

American Oldtime

LITTLE BURNT POTATO

Arr. by S.J.Hawley
Learned from Jane and Bill Kuhlman, Michigan

New England Traditional

LOGGERMAN'S BREAKDOWN

Arr. by S. J. Hawley

New England Traditional

Learned from Paul Van Arsdale

LOGGERMAN'S BREAKDOWN
(Accompaniment)

Arr. by S. J. Hawley

New England Traditional

LOG CABIN WALTZ

Arr. by S. J. Hawley

Oldtime Traditional Waltz

84

LOST INDIAN

Oldtime Traditional
Learned from Lefty Shafer

Arr. by S. J. Hawley

MAGPIE

Arr. by S. J. Hawley
Learned from Joe Dobbs

Oldtime Traditional

MICKEY CHEWING BUBBLEGUM

Arr. by S. J. Hawley
Learned from Jack Barclay

Oldtime Traditional Polka

MISSISSIPPI SAWYER

Arr. by S. J. Hawley
Learned from Ray Epler

Oldtime Traditional

Sally Hawley and Ray Epler, Footmad Festival, Camp Shepherd, Roane Co., West Virginia.

Ray Epler, Sally Hawley, Buddy Koontz

NORWEGIAN GIRL

Arr. by S. J. Hawley
Learned from Ray Epler

Traditional

OLD FRENCH

Arr. by S.J.Hawley

Traditional Hornpipe

OLD GREY CAT ON A TENNESSEE FARM

Arr. by S. J. Hawley

Oldtime Traditional

OLD JOE CLARK

Arr. by S.J.Hawley

American Traditional

With Embellishments:

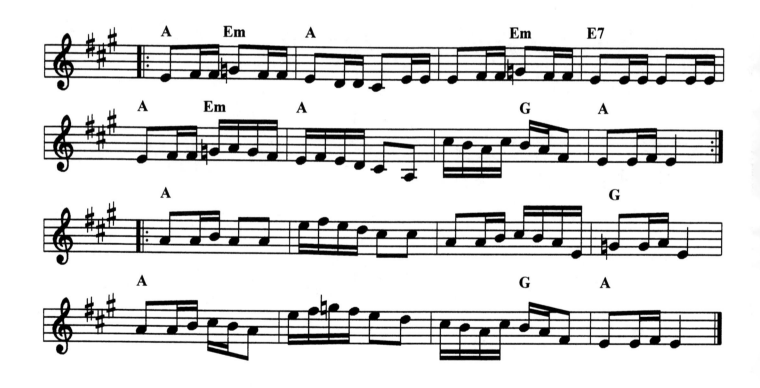

OLD MOLLY HARE

Arr. by S. J. Hawley

Oldtime and Scots Traditional

ON THE ROAD TO BOSTON

Arr. by S. J. Hawley
Nice as a round.

Traditional Tune

Vandalia Gathering, WV State Cultural Center, Charleston, West Virginia.

OVER THE WATERFALL

Arr. by S. J. Hawley

Oldtime Traditional

PEACOCK RAG

Arr. by S.J.Hawley
Learned from Worley Gardner

Arthur Smith
Oldtime Traditional

PENNY CANDY

S. J. Hawley

Memories of growing up in the 1930s
during the depression years.

Oh, I was so good, did as I should, and kept my smile right
There were sug - ar straws, break - ers of jaws, that'd give a day of

han - dy, Did my chores all day, and got my pay, to
trou - ble; There were lem - on drops and sug - ar pops, or

buy some pen - ny can - dy! Oh, the cho - ices there would
gum to chew or bub - ble! Or some pep - per mint or

curl your hair: Guess - whats with toys and kiss - es, There were
lico - rice sticks, and pea - nuts fresh and crunch - y, or

choc - o - let bars, marsh - mal - low stars, lolly pops and oth - er
se - ven goo - ey cara - mel squares, and co - co - nut so

blis - ses! - Oh, we'd skip and hop to the can - dy shop, Oh the
mun - chy!

times, they we - re so dan - dy! Oh, it made work play, and a

hap - - py day, just a piece of pen - ny can - dy!

98

PETRONELLA

Arr. by S. J. Hawley

Oldtime Traditional

Vandalia Gathering, WV State Cultural Center, Charleston, West Virginia.

PIGTOWN FLING

Arr. by S. J. Hawley
Learned from Diane McIntyre

Oldtime and Irish Traditional Reel
Also called "Stoney Creek"

POLLY, PUT THE KETTLE ON

Arr. by S. J. Hawley

Oldtime Traditional

POSSUM UP A GUM STUMP

Arr. by S. J. Hawley
Augusta Heritage Class

American Traditional

PRAIRIE FLOWER

Arr. by S. J. Hawley
Learned from Patty Looman

Oldtime Traditional

WV State Folk Festival, Conrad Motel, Glenville, West Virginia.

103

PRETTY LITTLE DOG

Arr. by S. J. Hawley

Oldtime Traditional

WV State Folk Festival, High Times at the Conrad, Glenville, West Virginia.

PUNCHEON FLOOR

Arr. by S. J. Hawley

Oldtime Traditional Reel

Jam at the Coffee Shop, WV State Folk Festival, Glenville, West Virginia.

PUT ON YOUR OLD GRAY BONNET

Arr. by S. J. Hawley
Learned from Nova Hunter, Ray Epler, and Russell Fluharty

Oldtime Traditional

On the old farm house ver-an-da there sat Si-las and Mir-an-da, think-ing

of the days gone by; He said "dear-y don't be wear-y, you were

al-ways bright and cheer-y, but a tear, dear, dims your eye". She said

"they're not tears of sad-ness, Si las, they are tears of glad-ness, it's been.

fif-ty years to-day that we were wed!" - Then his dim old eyes were bright-ened, and his

tired old heart was light-ened, as he turned to her and said,.

"Put on your old gray bon-net, with the blue ribb-ons on it, while I

hitch old Dobb-in to the shay; - Thru the fields of clo-ver, we'll ride

o'er to Dov-er, on our Gold-en Wed-ding Day!"

THE QUILTING PARTY

Arr. by S. J. Hawley

American Traditional

In the sky the bright stars glit - tered, On the

bank the pale moon shone; and 'twas from Aunt Din - ah's

quilt - ing par - ty I was see - ing Nel - lie home. I was

see - ing Nel - lie ho - me, I was see - ing Nel - lie

home, And 'twas from Aunt Din - ah's quilt - ing par - ty I was

see - ing Nel - lie home. home.

RAGTIME ANNIE

Arr. by S. J. Hawley

Oldtime Traditional Reel

Part A:

RAGTIME ANNIE

Oldtime Traditional

109

RACHEL

Arr. by S.J.Hawley

Traditional

Alternate Part B:

RED APPLE RAG

Arr. by S. J. Hawley

Oldtime Traditional

RED WING

Arr. by S. J. Hawley

Oldtime Traditional

RICKETT'S HORNPIPE

Arr. by S.J.Hawley

Oldtime Traditional

RUNNING THE RAPIDS

S. J. Hawley
New River Rafting and Kayaking

Oldtime Style

SANDY RIVER BELLE

Arr. by S. J. Hawley

Oldtime Traditional

SIMPLE GIFTS

Arr. by S. J. Hawley

Traditional Shaker Hymn

SOLDIER'S JOY

Arr. by S.J.Hawley

Traditional

SOURWOOD MOUNTAIN

Arr. by S. J. Hawley

Traditional Oldtime

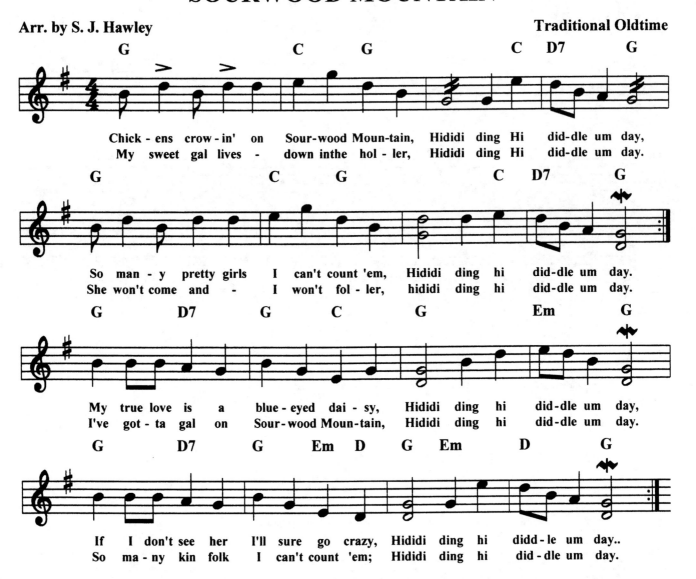

Chick - ens crow - in' on Sour-wood Moun-tain, Hididi ding Hi did-dle um day,
My sweet gal lives - down in the hol - ler, Hididi ding Hi did-dle um day.

So man - y pretty girls I can't count 'em, Hididi ding hi did-dle um day.
She won't come and - I won't fol - ler, hididi ding hi did-dle um day.

My true love is a blue - eyed dai - sy, Hididi ding hi did-dle um day,
I've got - ta gal on Sour-wood Moun-tain, Hididi ding hi did-dle um day.

If I don't see her I'll sure go crazy, Hididi ding hi didd-le um day..
So ma - ny kin folk I can't count 'em; Hididi ding hi did-dle um day.

Variation:

SPARROW IN THE TREE TOP

Arr. by S. J. Hawley

Oldtime Schottische

STATEN ISLAND HORNPIPE

Arr. by S.J.Hawley

New England Traditional

Carnegie Hall campus, "A Taste of Lewisburg", Lewisburg, West Virginia.

SWEET SIXTEEN

Arr. by S. J. Hawley
Also called "Too Young To Marry"

Oldtime/Scots Traditional
Scots name, "My Love Is But A Lassie"

TEMPERANCE REEL

Arr. by S. J. Hawley

Oldtime Traditional

TURKEY IN THE STRAW

Arr. by S. J. Hawley

Oldtime Traditional Reel

TWENTY-EIGHTH OF JANUARY

Arr. by S. J. Hawley

Oldtime Traditional

124

TWIN SISTERS

Arr. by S. J. Hawley

Oldtime Traditional

Learned from Bill Smith at W.Va.State Folk Festival, Glenville, WV.

THE VIRGINIA REEL

Arr. by S. J. Hawley

Oldtime Traditional

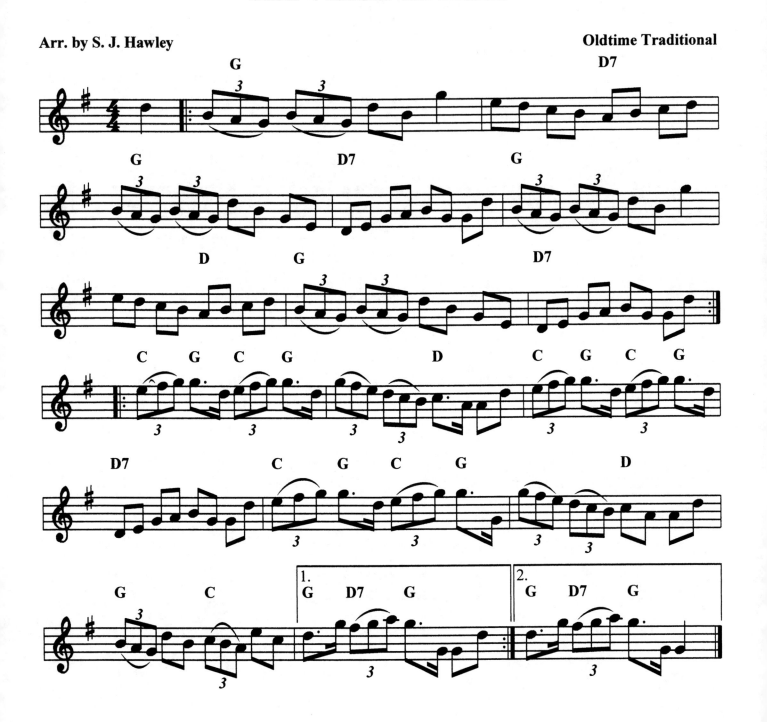

WATERBOUND

Arr. by S. J. Hawley

WEST FORK GIRLS

Arr. by S. J. Hawley

West Virginia Traditional

WESTPHALIA WALTZ

Arr. by S. J. Hawley
(The Never Fail-ya Waltz)

Oldtime Traditional
A coast to coast favorite

WHEN WE GO DOWN TO WASHINGTON

Arr. by S. J. Hawley

American Fife Tune

WHISKEY BEFORE BREAKFAST

Arr. by S. J. Hawley

WHISTLING RUFUS

Arr. by S.J.Hawley

Oldtime Traditional

WHITE COCKADE

Arr. by S. J. Hawley

Traditional Oldtime and Celtic Reel

133

THE YEAR OF JUBILO

Arr. by S. J. Hawley

Oldtime Traditional

Section 2
Celtic Traditional Tunes

AM COMBRA DUNN HORNPIPE

Arr. by S. J. Hawley

Traditional Irish

THE ASH GROVE

Arr. by S. J. Hawley

Welsh Traditional Waltz

THE ATHOLL HIGHLANDERS

Arr. by S. J. Hawley

Traditional Scots March

138

THE BLARNEY PILGRIM

Arr. by S. J. Hawley

Irish Traditional Jig

BLIND MARY

Arr. by S. J. Hawley

Turlough O'Carolan
Traditional Irish Aire

THE BOYS OF BLUEHILL

Arr. by S. J. Hawley

Irish Traditional Hornpipe

THE CAMPBELLS ARE COMING

Arr. by S. J. Hawley

Traditional Scottish Jig

Cabin Creek Quilts, Malden, West Virginia.

THE CAMPBELL'S FAREWELL TO REDGAP

Arr. by S. J. Hawley

Scots Traditional and Oldtime

CAPTAIN O'KANE

Arr. by S. J. Hawley

Turlough O'Carolan
Irish Traditional Aire

CARRICKFERGUS

Arr. by S. J. Hawley

Irish Traditional Aire

THE CASTLE OF DROMORE

Arr. by S. J. Hawley

8th Century Irish Lullaby

Introduction:

The Oct - o - ber winds - la - ment a-
Bring no ill winds to hin - der
Take time to thrive, my ray of

round the - Cast - le of Dro - more,
us; my - - help - less babe and me;
hope, in the gar - den of Dro - more,

- - Yet - peace is in her loft - y
Dread - spir - its of the black wat-
- - Take - heed, young eag - le till thy

halls, - my - lov - ing treas - ures store.
er, Clan - Ow - en's wild ban - shee,
wings are feathered and fit to soar.

THE CASTLE OF DROMORE
(Concluded)

8th Century Irish Lullaby

- - Though Aut - - umn leaves may fall and
- - And Ho - ly Ma - ry pi - ty - ing
- - A lit - - tle rest and then the

die a bud of Spring - are you.
us, in heaven for gra - ce doth sue.____
world, is full of work - to do.____

- Sing hush a by, loo - lah - loo - lah

lan, Sing hush - a - by loo - lah - loo____

____ Sing hush - a - by, loo - lah - loo.

SH' BHEAG SH'MOHR

Arr. by S. J. Hawley

Turlough O'Carolan
Irish Traditional Aire

CHARLIE HUNTER

Arr. by S. J. Hawley

Scots Traditional Jig

CHILDGROVE

Arr. by S. J. Hawley

English Traditional Aire

CLIFFS OF MOHER

Arr. by S. J. Hawley

Irish Traditional

THE COCK O' THE NORTH

Arr. by S. J. Hawley

British Isles Traditional

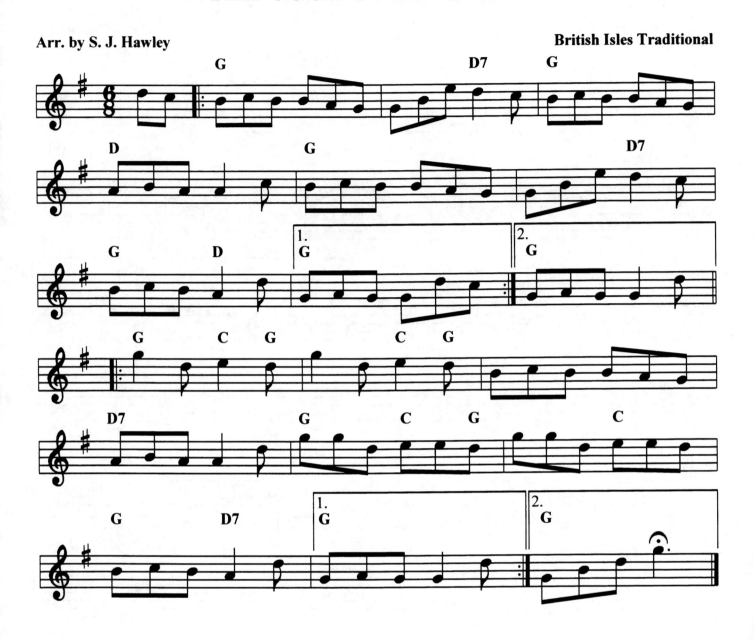

COOLEY'S REEL

Arr. by S. J. Hawley

Irish Traditional Reel

153

CRONIN'S HORNPIPE

Arr. by S. J. Hawley

Irish Traditional Hornpipe

THE CROSSES OF ANAGH

Arr. by S. J. Hawley
Learned from Tim Britain

Scots/Irish Traditional
Augusta Heritage Workshops

DONNYBROOK FAIR

Arr. by S. J. Hawley

Irish Traditional Jig

Vandalia Gathering, WV State Cultural Center, Capitol Grounds, Charleston, West Virginia.

DOWN IN THE BRAE

Arr. by S. J. Hawley
Learned from Michael Petersen

Scottish Traditional

DROWSY MAGGIE

Arr. by S. J. Hawley

Irish Traditional Reel

DUNPHY'S HORNPIPE

Arr. by S. J. Hawley
Learned from David Gladkosky

Irish Traditional

EIBH'I GHEAL CHU'IN NI CH'EARBAIL

Ancient Gaelic Aire

Arr. by S. J. Hawley
Learned from Micheal Fries

FAIRY DANCE

Arr. by S. J. Hawley

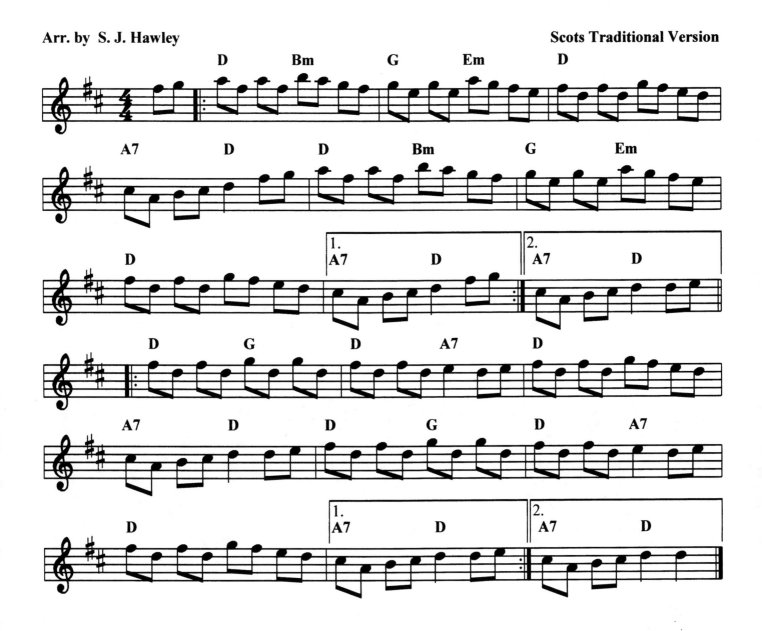

FLOWERS OF EDINBURGH

Arr. by S. J. Hawley

Scottish and Oldtime Traditional Reel

GILDEROY
(Little Red Haired Boy)

Arr. by S. J. Hawley

Irish Traditional Reel

163

GILDEROY
(The Little Red Haired Boy)

Arr. by S. J. Hawley
With Embellishments

Arr. by S. J. Hawley

Irish Traditional

THE GIRL I LEFT BEHIND ME

Arr. by S. J. Hawley

Ancient Gaelic Reel

THE GRASSY TURF

Arr. by S. J. Hawley

Turlough O'Carolan
Scots/Irish Traditional

GREENSLEEVES

Arr. by S. J. Hawley

Traditional English Aire

THE HALTING MARCH

Arr. by S. J. Hawley

Irish Traditional

Prickett's Fort State Park Traditional Music Festival, Fairmont, West Virginia.

Sally Hawley and Peggy Strang, Roscoe Village Dulcimer Festival, Coshocton, Ohio.

HASTE TO THE WEDDING

Arr. by S. J. Hawley

Irish Traditional

Cabin Creek Quilts, Malden, West Virginia.

THE HIGHLAND FLING

Arr. by S. J. Hawley

Scots Traditional

HIGHLAND LADDIE

Arr. by S. J. Hawley

Scots Traditional

THE HIGH LEVEL HORNPIPE

Arr. by S. J. Hawley

James Hill, 19th Century, Northern England

THE HUNDRED PIPERS

Arr. by S. J. Hawley

Scots Traditional

Drone B and F together for Introduction

Wi' a hun - dred pi - pers an - aye an - aye, Wi' a hun - dred pi - pers an-
A th' sod - jer la - ds, they looked bra looked, Wi' thr tar - tans, kil - ts an-
O a tis the fore - maist o' - aye o' aye, - O what does fol - low the.
Wi' - wounds sae swoll - en sae red, an'sae deep, But - shoder to sho-der th'

aye, an - aye, We' - ll up an' gie' them a' blaw, a' blaw, Wi' a
aye, an - aye, Wi' - bonnets and feath - ers an' glitt - ring gear, An'
blaw, the blaw? Bon - ny Charlie the king of us aye' hur - rah! Wi' his.
brave lads keep, Ten - thousand - swam to fell Eng - lish ground, An'

hun - dred pi - pers an' aye, an' aye, Oh its ow - er the bor - der a'
pibrochs - sou - nd - ing sweet an' clear, Wi - ll a' - re - turn to their
hun - dred pi - pers an' aye, an' aye! His - bon - net and feath - ers he's
danced'm'selves - dry to the pi - brochs sound. Dis - - found - ered the Eng - lish they

wae, a' wae, Its - ow - er the bor - der a' wae, a' wae, We' - ll
own dear glen? Wi - ll they a' come - back our high - land men? Second
wav - in high! His - pranc - in' steed - maist - seems to fly! The -
saw, they saw, Dis - foundered - they - heard the blaw, the blaw! Dis -

174

THE HUNDRED PIPERS
(Concluded)

Scots Traditional

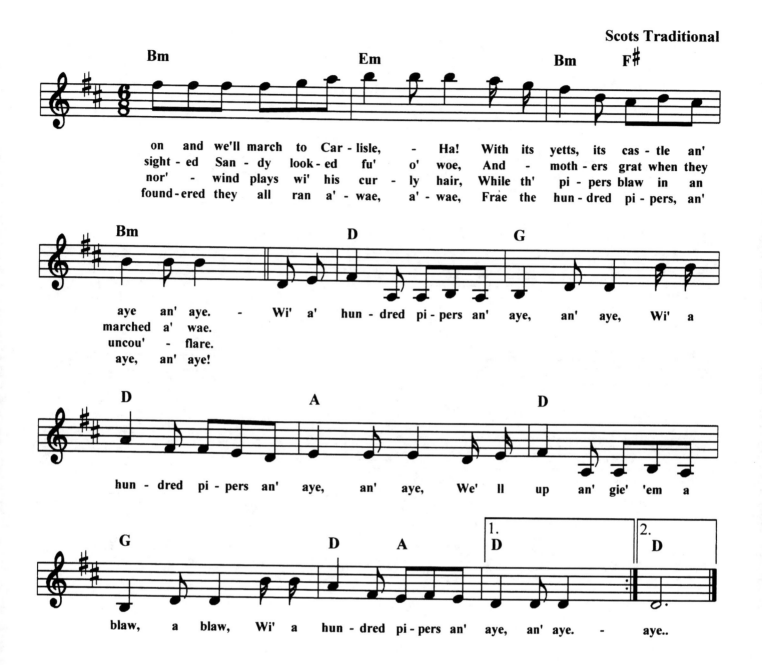

on and we'll march to Car-lisle, - Ha! With its yetts, its cas-tle an'
sight-ed San-dy look-ed fu' o' woe, And - moth-ers grat when they
nor' - wind plays wi' his cur-ly hair, While th' pi-pers blaw in an
found-ered they all ran a'-wae, a'-wae, Frae the hun-dred pi-pers, an'

aye an' aye. - Wi' a' hun-dred pi-pers an' aye, an' aye, Wi' a
marched a' wae.
uncou' - flare.
aye, an' aye!

hun-dred pi-pers an' aye, an' aye, We'll up an' gie' 'em a

blaw, a blaw, Wi' a hun-dred pi-pers an' aye, an' aye. - aye..

THE HUNTER'S HORNPIPE

Arr. by S.J.Hawley

Irish/Scots Traditional

IF I HAD MAGGIE IN THE WOODS

Arr. by S. J. Hawley
Learned from Michael Fries

Irish Traditional

I'LL TELL ME MA

Arr. by S. J. Hawley
Learned from Terry Manshiem

Irish Traditional

IN THE SALLY GARDENS

Arr. by S. J. Hawley

Irish Traditional Aire

INVERNESS GATHERING

Arr. by S. J. Hawley

Traditional Scots

ISABELLA BURKE

Arr. by S. J. Hawley

Turlough O'Carolan
Scots/Irish Aire

JAMIE ALLEN

Arr. by S. J. Hawley

Traditional Tune

JENNY DANG THE WEAVER

Arr. by S. J. Hawley

Irish Traditional

JIG OF SLURS

Arr. by S. J. Hawley

Irish Traditional Jig

JOHN RYAN'S POLKA

Arr. by S. J. Hawley
Learned from Larry Spizak

Irish Traditional

THE KERRY DANCERS

Arr. by S. J. Hawley

Irish Traditional

KERRY FLING

Arr. S.J.Hawley

Irish Traditional

KESH JIG

Arr.by S.J.Hawley

Irish Traditional

KITTY'S WEDDING

Arr. by S.J.Hawley
Learned from Harriet Peters

Irish Traditional Hornpipe
This is also nice as an aire

189

LA BASTRANGUE

Arr. by S.J.Hawley
Learned from Kathy O'Hanlon

French Traditional

LANNIGAN'S BALL

Arr. by S.J.Hawley

Irish Traditional

LASS OF PEATY'S MILL

Arr. by S.J.Hawley

Scots Traditional

LOCH LAVAN CASTLE

Arr. by S.J.Hawley

British Isles Traditional

MACHYNLETH

Arr. by S. J. Hawley
Learned from Harriet Peters

Welsh Traditional

194

THE MAID BEHIND THE BAR

Arr. by S. J. Hawley

Irish Traditional Reel

MARI'S WEDDING

Arr. by S. J. Hawley

British Isles Traditional Polka

THE MARQUIS OF HUNTLEY

Arr. by S. J. Hawley

Traditional Strathspey

MASON'S APRON

Arr. by S. J. Hawley

Irish Traditional

MC CUSKERS DELIGHT

Arr. by S.J.Hawley
Learned from John Goodman

Scots Traditional Hornpipe

MC KINNON BROOK

Arr. by S. J. Hawley
Learned from Mike Petersen

Scots Traditional

THE MERRY BLACKSMITH

Arr. by S. J. Hawley

Irish Traditional Reel
Also known as "Paddy On The Railroad"

Jamming with the Merry Blacksmith, Ron Utt, at Prickett's Fort
Traditional Music weekend, Fairmont, West Virginia.

THE MINSTREL BOY

Arr. by S. J. Hawley

British Isles Traditional

MISS MC LEOD'S REEL

Arr. by S. J. Hawley

Scots Traditional Reel
Also known as "Hop High Ladies"

MISS MOORE'S RANT

Arr. by S. J. Hawley

English Country Dance

MONAGHAN'S JIG

Arr. by S. J. Hawley

Irish Traditional Jig

MONEY MUSK

Arr. by S. J. Hawley

Ancient Celtic Reel

MORE POWER TO YOUR ELBOW

Arr. by S.J.Hawley

Irish Traditional

THE MORNING OF LIFE

Arr. by S. J. Hawley

Turlough O'Carolan
Irish Traditional Aire

MORRISON'S JIG

Arr. by S. J. Hawley

Irish Traditional

209

THE MUSICAL PRIEST

Arr. by S. J. Hawley

Irish Traditional

MY LOVE IS BUT A LASSIE

Arr. by S. J. Hawley

Oldtime/Scots Traditional
American version called "Sweet Sixteen"
or "Too Young To Marry"

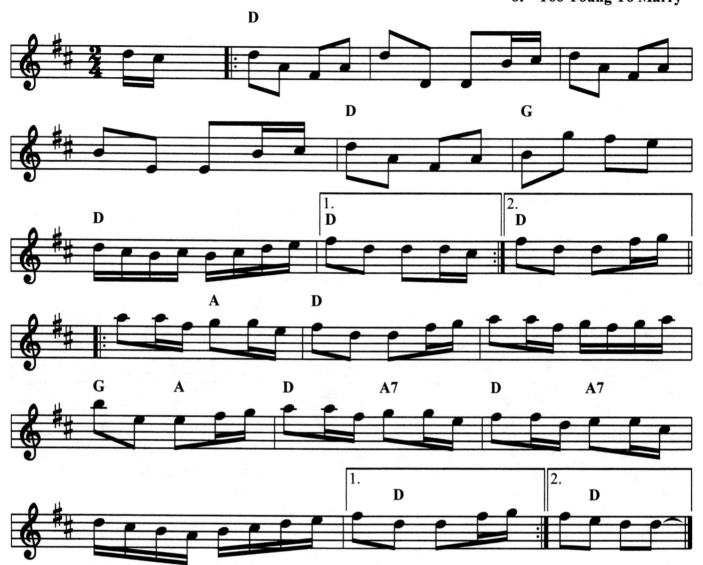

NED OF THE HILL

Arr. by S. J. Hawley

Irish Traditional Aire

NEW RIGGED SHIP

Arr. by S. J. Hawley

Scots Traditional Reel

THE NIGHTINGALE

Arr. by S. J. Hawley

English Traditional Waltz
Also known as "One Morning In May"

In Key of D:

O'CAROLAN'S DREAM

Arr. by S. J. Hawley

Turlough O'Carolan
18th Century Irish Harpist

215

O'DONNELL'S HORNPIPE

Arr. by S.J.Hawley

Irish Traditional

OFF TO CALIFORNIA

Arr. by S.J.Hawley

Irish Traditional

Alternate Part B:

17

OLD MAN DILLON

Arr. by S. J. Hawley

Irish Traditional Jig

ORANGE AND BLUE JIG

Arr. by S. J. Hawley

Irish Traditional Jig

THE OULD ORANGE FLUTE

Arr. by S. J. Hawley

Irish Traditional
Americanized as "Sweet Betsy From Pike"

PADDY ON THE RAILROAD

Arr. by S. J. Hawley

Irish Traditional Reel
Also called "The Merry Blacksmith"

PADDY ON THE TURNPIKE

Arr. by S. J. Hawley

Irish Traditional Reel

PADDY O'RAFFERTY

Arr. by S. J. Hawley

Irish Traditional Jig

PADDY WHACK

Arr. by S. J. Hawley

Traditional Irish Jig

PIPE ON THE HOB

Arr. by S. J. Hawley
Learned from Wendell Dobbs

Irish Traditional Jig

PLANXTY DREW

Arr. by S. J. Hawley

Irish Traditional
Turlough O'Carolan

PLANXTY FANNY POWER

Arr. by S. J. Hawley

Turlough O'Carolan
Irish Traditonal Aire

PLANXTY IRWIN

Arr. by S. J. Hawley

Turlough O'Carolan
Irish Traditional

PLANXTY MAGGIE BROWN

Arr. by S. J. Hawley

Turlough O'Carolan
Irish Traditional Jig

229

RIGHTS OF MAN

Arr. by S. J. Hawley

THE ROAD TO LISDOONVARNA

Arr. by S. J. Hawley

Traditional Irish Jig

THE ROSE TREE

Arr. by S. J. Hawley

Scots/Irish Traditional

SAINT ANNE'S REEL

Arr. by S. J. Hawley

Oldtime and Celtic Traditional

SAINT KILDA'S WEDDING

Arr. by S. J. Hawley

Scots/Irish Traditional Polka

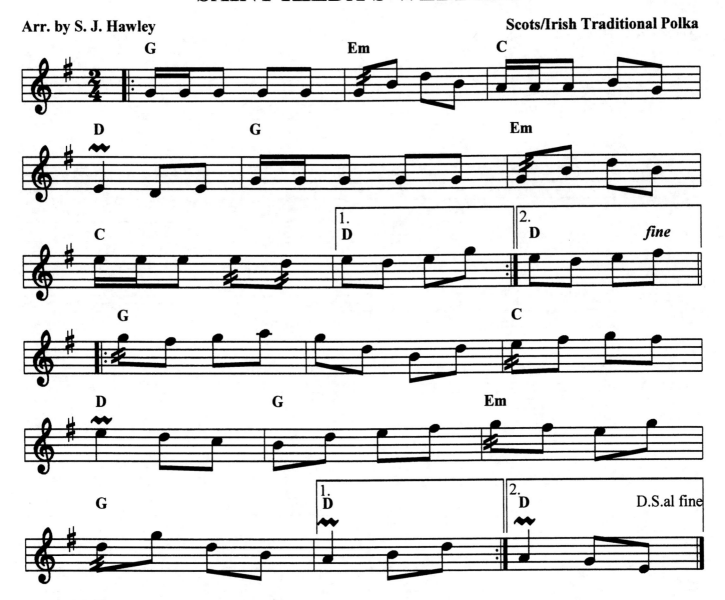

SAINT PATRICK'S DAY IN THE MORNING

Arr. by S. J. Hawley

Traditional Irish Jig

SALLY HUNTER OF THURSTON

Arr. by S. J. Hawley

Scots Traditional Jig

THE SCHOLAR

Arr. by S. J. Hawley

British Isles Traditional

SCOTLAND THE BRAVE

Arr. by S. J. Hawley

Scots Traditional March

SCOTS MIST

Arr. by S. J. Hawley

Scots Traditional

SEAMUS O'BRIEN

Arr. by S. J. Hawley

Irish Traditional Aire

THE SILVER SPEAR

Arr. by S. J. Hawley

Irish Traditional Reel

SLIGO FANCY

Arr. by S.J.Hawley

Irish Traditional

SOUTHWIND

Arr. by S. J. Hawley

Ancient Gaelic Aire

SPANCIL HILL

Arr. by S. J. Hawley

Irish Traditional Aire

SPINNING WHEEL TUNES MEDLEY

Arr. by S. J. Hawley

Ancient Irish Traditional

STACK OF BARLEY

Arr. by S. J. Hawley

Irish Traditional Hornpipe

STAR OF MUNSTER

Arr. by S. J. Hawley

Irish Traditional Reel

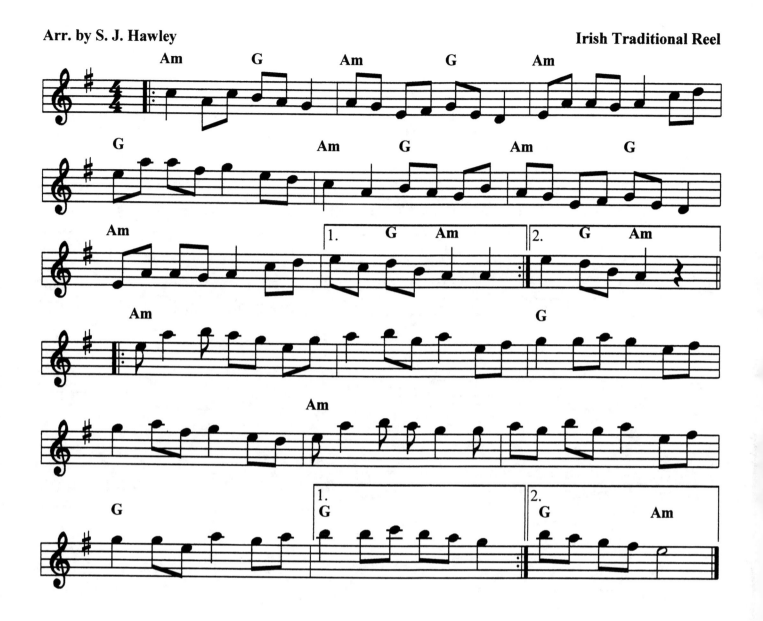

SWALLOWTAIL JIG

Arr. by S. J. Hawley

Irish Traditional Jig

SWEET RICHARD

Arr. by S. J. Hawley

English Country Dance - 1742

TEMPERANCE REEL

Arr. by S. J. Hawley

Oldtime and Irish Traditional

TEN PENNY BIT

Arr. by S. J. Hawley

Irish Traditional Jig

TOBIN'S JIG

Arr. by S. J. Hawley

Irish Traditional Jig

THE TOP O' CORK ROAD

Arr. by S. J. Hawley
Learned from Don Udell

Irish Traditional Jig
Also called "Father Flanagan"

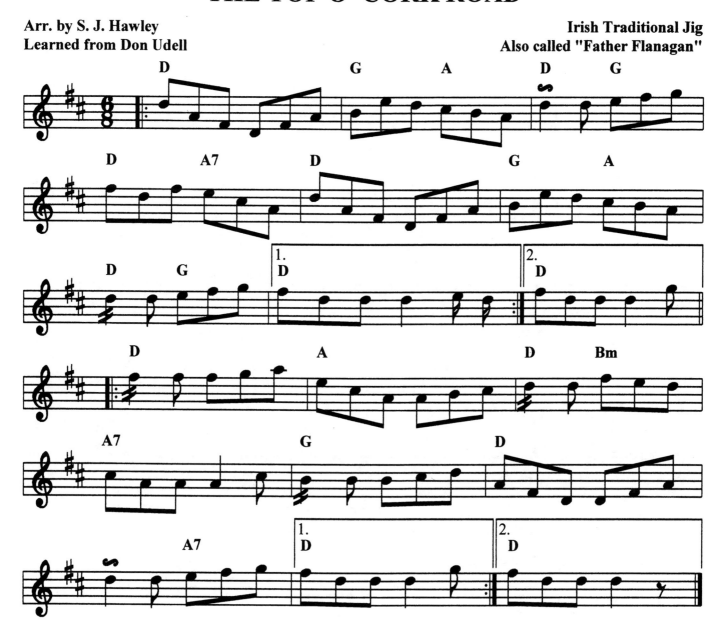

THE TOUCHSTONE

Arr. by S. J. Hawley

English Country Dance Tune

TRIP TO SLIGO

Arr. by S.J.Hawley

Irish Traditional

THE WEAVERS

Arr. by S. J. Hawley

Irish Traditional Slide